THE
UNICORN'S SECRET

#4

The Mountains
of the Moon

by Kathleen Duey

illustrated by Omar Rayyan

ALADDIN

New York   London   Toronto   Sydney   Singapore

For all the daydreamers . . .

This book is a work of fiction. Any references to historical events, real people, or real locales are used fictitiously. Other names, characters, places, and incidents are the product of the author's imagination, and any resemblance to actual events or locales or persons, living or dead, is entirely coincidental.

First Aladdin edition July 2002
Text copyright © 2002 by Kathleen Duey
Illustrations copyright © 2002 by Omar Rayyan

Aladdin Paperbacks
An imprint of Simon & Schuster
Children's Publishing Division
1230 Avenue of the Americas
New York, NY 10020

Also available in an Aladdin library edition.
Designed by Debra Sfetsios
The text of this book was set in Golden Cockerel ITC.
Manufactured in the United States of America
10 9

ISBN-13: 978-0-689-84272-6
ISBN-10: 0-689-84272-4
Library of Congress Control Number for the Library Edition 2002104397
0910 OFF

The Gypsies know Moonsilver is a real unicorn now—and the people in Derrytown will soon figure it out. It won't be long before Lord Dunraven's men are searching for the Gypsies. Now more than ever Heart needs a safe place, a home.

+CHAPTER ONE

Heart led the way through the midnight forest.

Moon shadows striped the ground.

Kip trotted close beside Avamir, his ears high, his tail raised like a flag.

Behind Heart, Moonsilver blew out a long, soft breath. He touched her shoulder lightly with his muzzle.

As they started walking downhill Heart sighed, thinking about the silver bracelet on her wrist.

How had the silver threads woven themselves together?

Was it magic?

What else could it be?

A whisper of breeze touched the treetops.

Heart looked up at the full moon, then back at the rocky hillside. They had to hide.

But *where?*

Heart shifted the carry-sack on her back. Where were the moon-colored mountains she had dreamed about? Were they real? She shook her head. Chasing dreams would hardly help.

Heart tried to remember what Binney had told her.

"To the west is Lord Irmaedith," Heart whispered to herself.

She knew nothing about Lord Irmaedith.

Was he cruel?

Worse than Lord Dunraven?

"And to the East, it's Lord Kaybale," Heart said aloud, repeating Binney's words.

Lord Kaybale.

She had never heard of him, either.

No one in Ash Grove had known anything about the world beyond the village. No one ever talked about it. Not even Ruth Oakes.

In the moonlit dusk ahead a boulder took

shape, rising out of the ground as big as a farmer's house.

Heart led the unicorns around it.

The dry pine needles crumbled beneath her feet and the unicorns' hooves, scenting the still night air.

Heart could hear Kip's quick, panting breath.

At least he was excited about this journey. No one else could be.

Ruth would be so worried.

Heart's Gypsy friends would be sad when they discovered she was gone.

But Binney and Zim would understand, Heart knew. They would know that she didn't want to bring them trouble.

"I am afraid," Heart breathed, glancing down at the silver bracelet on her wrist.

The six silver threads were now a lacy circle.

"They tell the story of my life," Heart whispered to herself. "Or as much of it as I can remember."

It was true. Two had come from the blanket

she'd been wrapped in when Simon found her by the Blue River.

One was a gift from dear Ruth Oakes.

Three were from Binney in thanks for Moonsilver saving Davey's life.

Heart stared at the intricate woven pattern in the bracelet.

Binney had said her threads were from the Queen of the Unicorns' mane.

Heart glanced at Avamir.

The white mare was beautiful, and her mane was long and silky. But it was white, not silver.

So maybe that part wasn't true?

Avamir tossed her head.

The tiny Gypsy bells in her mane jingled against the vast silence of the forest, then stilled.

Heart felt Moonsilver's muzzle against her shoulder, another quick, warm touch. She wished desperately that she knew what to do, where to go. Derrytown was on the edge of Lord Dunraven's lands—his castle lay somewhere to the north. He would be the first to hear the rumors about Moonsilver healing Davey.

"Lord Kaybale," she said aloud, trying to break the panic-circle of her thoughts. "Lord Kaybale is to the East."

Heart liked the rounded, strong sound of the name Kaybale.

It was plain and sturdy.

It sounded like an everyday word—like *rainwater* or *hearthstone*. But Lord Kaybale's lands lay to the East of Lord Dunraven's—beyond Ash Grove.

Heart was afraid to go back that way.

Lord Dunraven's men would search there first. He would send his men to watch the Derrytown Road and the village—and Ruth Oakes's house.

Heart took a deep breath.

Everyone in Ash Grove had heard the old stories about the unicorn and the Blue River.

But no one had thought unicorns were *real*.

Now the rumors would spread. They would wonder. They would watch.

"Where can we go?" Heart asked the sky.

Northward was Lord Dunraven's manor. Southward lay Lord Levin's lands, according to Binney.

North, south, east, west.

There was no reason to think any direction led to safety.

Heart felt a familiar ache rising inside her.

Her family might help her—if she could find them.

But she had no idea where they were—or even *who* they were.

A rustling sound up the slope made Heart turn.

She caught her breath.

A vague shape was slipping in and out of the moon shadows.

Someone—or something—was at the top of the slope, following her.

✦CHAPTER TWO

*A*head in the moonlight Heart saw another huge boulder. She hurried the unicorns toward it.

Kip trotted beside her.

"Shhh," she whispered to him.

Kip's eyes were bright. He lifted his muzzle. He did not bark.

The unicorns moved almost silently. Heart walked carefully, leading Moonsilver and Avamir around to the far side of the huge stone.

She set down her carry-sack.

Kip and the unicorns stood close together in the deep shadows cast by the enormous boulder.

After a few moments Heart heard footsteps coming closer.

She could hear a voice, too.

It was so familiar her stomach turned over.

Simon? What was *Simon Pratt* doing here?

Avamir breathed out, lifting her head.

"He might offer me silver on the spot," Simon was saying to himself as he came closer.

Heart pressed herself against the rock. The stone was rough and hard beneath her hands. What was *he* doing this far from Ash Grove?

"Or he might be angry," Simon was muttering. "But at Ruth Oakes, not at me. . . ."

Heart strained to hear more, but the sound of Simon's voice and footfalls dimmed, then disappeared. He hadn't seen her.

"Who will be angry?" Heart breathed.

Moonsilver tossed his head.

Kip was looking up at Heart.

Shivering with dread, she waited until Simon was well ahead of them, then she followed. Kip stayed at her heels. The unicorns were graceful and quiet as always.

Simon never looked back.

He kept muttering to himself.

Heart was afraid to get close enough to understand what he was saying. She glanced at the moon.

It was shining low through the trees on her left.

She caught her breath.

The moon *set* in the west.

That meant the road had curved northward—the direction of Lord Dunraven's castle.

Was that where Simon was headed?

Heart felt numb. Simon was afraid of Lord Dunraven. Everyone was. Why would Simon be walking toward the castle in the middle of the night like this?

She could think of only one reason.

He had heard the rumors.

He had figured out the truth.

Now he was going to tell Lord Dunraven all he knew about her, about Ruth Oakes . . . and about the unicorns.

"You will have to hide and wait for me," Heart whispered to Avamir.

The unicorn mare lifted her head. Her eyes were calm.

Heart veered off the road and found a rocky point.

In the distance she could just see the high walled castle. Beyond it rose steep mountains that disappeared into the night sky.

"Stay hidden," Heart pleaded with Kip. "Stay here with Moonsilver and Avamir."

She set down her carry-sack on the rocky ground.

There was a tiny clinking sound.

Her flute!

"Dear Zim," Heart breathed. What a gift he had given her, teaching her to play. Maybe one day she would find a way to repay the Gypsies for all their kindness.

Kip whined softly.

Avamir blew out a disapproving breath and Kip sat down and hushed. Moonsilver moved uneasily. Heart put her hand on his neck for an instant.

"I'll be back as quickly as I can," she promised them all.

Avamir shook her mane.

The silvery jingle of the Gypsy bells made Heart sigh.

Heart hugged Avamir's silky neck and patted Kip's head.

Then she set off.

Once she was back down on the road, Heart couldn't see the castle.

There was a village along the road.

Heart had heard stories about it. She had always wanted to see what might be sold in such fancy shops for lords and ladies.

Now she was only glad no lanterns were lit.

All was dark. She couldn't see into the shops.

But no one could see her either—and she was grateful.

+CHAPTER THREE

Heart trailed behind Simon, keeping him in sight and trying to think of a way to talk him out of betraying her.

She could promise him money, but Lord Dunraven might reward him a thousand times more than she could ever earn.

She could plead with him—but she was pretty sure he would not listen. He might even force her to go with him to Lord Dunraven's castle.

Heart followed silently, unsure what she could do.

But she had to try *something*.

Simon was still muttering to himself.

Heart tried to get a little closer.

She heard Ruth's name once more, then her

own. He was rehearsing what he was going to say!

As they came around a bend in the road, Heart raised her head to call out to Simon.

Then she looked past him and caught her breath. Ahead in the dark, arched windows glowed with warm lantern light.

Dunraven's castle!

Shouts startled Heart.

She whirled and ran into the trees.

When she peeked out she could hear Simon's voice.

There were two men in dark shirts.

Lord Dunraven had guards on his road.

She crept closer.

"I just came to talk to Lord Dunraven," Simon was saying. He sounded scared.

Heart bit her lip.

"About what?" one guard demanded.

"I will tell *him* that," Simon insisted in a shaky voice.

"And what could a ragged field-gleaner

possibly know that our master does not?" the second guard scoffed.

Heart couldn't hear Simon's answer.

When the guards led him away, she followed.

She hid behind one tree, then another. She ducked under a wagon in a stable yard, waiting until the men were a little ahead of her.

The guards walked heavily, one on each side of Simon.

Heart stared at the castle as they got closer.

The bright moonlight traced its walls and towers with a silvery outline.

It was huge! It made the buildings in Derrytown seem as small as toys.

Dunraven's guards walked faster. They pushed Simon along.

Beyond the castle she could see mountains rising into the sky. Was that where the old road ran?

Binney had said it was ruined, that it had been closed for years and years.

Heart tried to keep close enough to hear what

Simon was saying, then realized he had fallen silent.

There was no sound except the guards' heavy boots on the gritty soil.

Around the castle there were no trees at all—nothing Heart could hide behind.

She stopped and watched as Dunraven's men led Simon along.

They headed straight for the castle wall.

Heart blinked. Where were they going?

One of the guards stepped forward and reached out. Heart couldn't see the round-topped door until it opened.

The guards marched Simon through the door.

Then it closed and it was impossible to see again. Heart was startled by the complete silence. There were no night birds here, no crickets. Even the sound of the guards' boots was gone.

The stone walls and towers stretched upward, taller than any tree.

Heart was afraid to move, but she made herself do it anyway.

She ran her hands along the stone wall, searching for the hidden door. She finally saw a tiny mark in the stone. When she touched it the door opened.

Heart squeezed inside and stood in a long corridor. Candlelight flickered dimly within.

Heart could see faint outlines of the wide arches leading into rooms on each side of a long hallway.

She could hear Simon's voice.

She took a step forward.

✦CHAPTER FOUR

"It is the truth," Simon was saying.

Heart slid along the cold stone wall, inching closer. The shadows piled along the walls, thick and ink-black.

"I found her by the river," Simon added in a trembling voice. "Raised her myself. Fed her from my hearth."

Heart's hands tightened. Simon was talking about *her*.

"There was a fancy blanket, but I . . . ," Simon began. He cleared his throat. "I sold it."

Heart peeked into the arched doorway.

There was a single candle on the table.

She was careful to stay in the darkness beyond the flickering light.

Simon was facing a tall man with long, silvery hair.

Heart knew him from that long-ago day in market square. It was Lord Dunraven. She held her breath.

Lord Dunraven gestured. One of the guards lit another candle. Lord Dunraven opened a massive wooden trunk.

He pulled out a child's blanket of fine woolen cloth.

Candlelight caught the silver embroidery.

The design was beautiful. There were two unicorns, rearing. Between them was a setting sun.

"That's it," Simon muttered. "But I sold it to a—"

"Bring him along," Dunraven said. His voice rumbled like summer thunder.

Heart felt her knees go weak. It was her blanket?

She twisted the bracelet on her wrist.

She wanted to leap out of the shadows and

take the blanket from Dunraven. She knew she couldn't.

Simon was cowering.

The guards held his arms.

Heart cringed backward into the dark shadows just as they turned.

She longed to see the blanket. *Her* blanket. She wanted to touch it.

Lord Dunraven led the way.

He carried a candle high.

Heart watched Simon and the guards follow him down the hallway.

She pressed her back against the stone wall, holding her breath. The amber candlelight was too weak to push the deep shadows aside. No one looked back. No one saw her crouching by the wall.

As the footsteps dimmed, Heart let out her breath.

She glanced down the corridor, back toward the round-topped door.

Then she risked a single step forward and

peeked in to the room where Dunraven and Simon had been.

It was filled with mysterious objects.

Heart glanced up the hall. She strained to listen.

The voices were distant now. There was no other sound.

She tiptoed into the room.

Candle shadows twitched and shivered; every breath of air moved the flames.

Heart struggled to open the trunk lid.

There were many things inside it, strange things for which she had no names. But her blanket was not there.

Lord Dunraven must have taken it with him.

Heart blinked back tears.

She looked around the room. There was a dark wooden table with legs carved in the shape of unicorns.

There was a set of shelves with bits of colored glass set into the wood.

Each shelf was full of peculiar, slender boxes.

Heart touched them.

They weren't boxes.

She pulled one out.

Two squares of dark leather enclosed a neat stack of paper.

Heart had seen Derrytown merchants figure sums on rough brown paper.

This was different. It was smooth and the color of cow's milk. It had rows of odd-shaped marks all over it—dark, perfect, tiny shapes.

Heart tugged at the top sheet.

The paper was fastened along one edge so it could not fall loose.

Heart turned over more leaves of the paper. The shapes were endless, like rows of ants marching after a rain.

Why would someone draw so many of the tiny designs?

They weren't even very pretty.

She turned two more leaves of the paper, then shook her head and flipped through the rest.

Something caught her eye, and she pressed the paper flat.

Heart exhaled slowly.

There was a drawing on the paper.

It showed two rearing unicorns with a sunset between them—exactly like the embroidery on her blanket.

Had this belonged to her family too?

Heart looked around the room again.

High on one wall there was a drawing of two unicorns, one white, one black.

Heart turned in a slow circle.

There was a cabinet with glass doors over the shelves. There were small carved statues of unicorns lined up inside. A carving of a long, slender unicorn horn lay in front of them. It looked like old oak. The tip was broken.

Heart shivered. She reached up to touch the glass. Her sleeve caught on the silver bracelet. It pinched her wrist. She dropped her arm to loosen her sleeve.

Then she bent down, staring through the glass.

The lowest shelf held a halter braided of thick golden cord.

"A reward?" The voice was sudden and deep. The words were followed by a harsh, deep laugh.

Lord Dunraven!

Heart heard heavy footsteps in the hallway.

She spun around and ran out of the room.

She fled down the corridor, staying bent over, keeping close to the wall, and hoping the shadows would hide her.

The round-topped door swung open easily.

The night air rushed in, cool and clean. Heart hesitated just long enough to glance back up the passage.

She could still hear muffled voices and the sound of heavy boots. Had they seen her?

She slipped outside and closed the door.

Then there was only the silence of the night.

Heart ran again, her pulse pounding in her throat. Every second she expected to hear angry shouts.

She ran until her lungs ached. The road

slanted uphill past the village, but she didn't slow down.

She was back to the trees before she realized she still had the strange paper box in her hand.

She stumbled to a halt and stared at it in the moonlight.

She *had* not meant to take it.

She wasn't a thief!

Would Lord Dunraven notice it was gone? Would he send his guards to find her?

Heart kicked at the ground, furious at herself.

If only she had put it back on the shelf! Lord Dunraven would never have known she'd been there.

But would he notice it was missing? The shelves had been full of paper boxes, and all of them had looked pretty much the same.

"I can only hope that he doesn't," Heart whispered to herself.

Around her the forest was deep and silent except for a silk-rustle breeze in the highest branches.

Heart was glad to be away from candles and dusty stone—back in the pure light of the moon.

She stood still, catching her breath.

Whatever Simon had told Lord Dunraven—and no matter how much of it Lord Dunraven had believed—men would soon be searching for her. Would they let Simon go home? Would Lord Dunraven give him a reward?

She would lead Kip and the unicorns westward tonight.

That was the quickest way out of Dunraven's lands.

She tightened her fists.

She would have taken the blanket if she'd been able to find it.

That blanket was *hers*.

Her mother and father had wrapped her in it and . . .

Heart's thoughts came to a stop, and she blinked back tears.

Simon Pratt had nearly stepped on her the

morning he had found her by the river. He had told her that much. The tall grass had nearly hidden her.

But why had she been left there? Heart wiped her eyes. It was so hard not knowing who her parents were.

She took a deep breath. The rearing unicorns were on her blanket and on the paper. For the first time, she had a clue that might lead to her family.

Heart squared her shoulders.

She would find them someday.

Her family would help her keep the unicorns safe.

But she would have to avoid Dunraven's men when they began to search.

Heart began to run again, light-footed with both hope and fear.

+CHAPTER FIVE

Ten days later, Heart was a long way from Dunraven's castle.

She had been very careful.

No one had spotted the unicorns.

Moonsilver and Avamir grazed beside forest streams. Heart had found berries and wild plums to eat. A farmer's wife had given her a mincemeat pie. Kip had caught mice and squirrels.

At first they had traveled by moonlight.

But the moon had waned now.

Traveling in the daytime, Heart stayed off the road. She led the unicorns and Kip through the forest alongside it.

She wanted to find a town.

She needed to earn a little money to buy food.

She wanted to show the drawing of the unicorns to people too. Maybe someone would recognize it.

"We have to find my family," she said out loud.

Avamir shook her mane. She reached out to touch her velvet muzzle to Heart's cheek. Her breath smelled of sweet grass.

Heart often caught glimpses of people passing on the road.

She saw a ladies' carriage, with matched bay horses snapping their hooves upward, necks arched.

There was a boy in rich clothing leading a horse.

Heart stared.

The horse's back and sides were covered with gray-silver metal.

Even its head was fitted with smooth silver.

A silver spike stuck out like a unicorn's horn. It had white plumes on it.

Heart had never seen a horse like this one. It was huge. Its hooves were broad as pie pans.

The next morning Heart heard something.

She listened, tipping her head to one side.

It was a rooster crowing. Later she heard a donkey bray.

There were farms up ahead.

That meant they were probably within a day's walk of a town.

Heart spent the morning heading uphill. They found a high valley with a thick stand of trees. There was a noisy stream and deep grass.

Avamir and Moonsilver would have to wait for her again. She hated to leave them, but if anyone saw them trouble would begin.

Heart kissed Avamir on the muzzle, then turned to Moonsilver. "You will stay hidden?"

Moonsilver's dark eyes were calm. Avamir switched her tail and arched her neck.

"Will you wait for me right here?" Heart asked her.

The mare lifted her head and looked at Heart. Heart knew they both understood. They would stay out of sight.

But Kip ran in circles around her legs.

Heart laughed softly. "You can come, but you have to be good."

Kip barked once, a high, happy sound. He sat down, thumping his tail.

Heart lifted her carry-sack. Kip watched her, his eyes bright. When she began to walk he leaped after her. Together they made their way back down the steep hillside.

The road was wide and level. There were thousands of wheel ruts. There was a jumble of cloven tracks, hoof prints, and boot marks.

Far ahead Heart saw a farmer's wagon. But no one was close enough to see her step out of the forest.

The sun was warm.

Billowing clouds drifted across the sky.

Heart smiled as she walked. It was a fine, wide road.

Coming around bend, Heart noticed something lying in the dirt.

She picked it up.

"A goat's horn?" she wondered aloud.

Kip sniffed at it. He tried to take it from her.

"No," Heart said firmly.

She shuddered, pitying the goat, thinking about the scar on Avamir's face.

Kip whined, wagging his tail.

Heart knew he would chew it like he would a bone.

She ran her fingers over the long, smooth horn.

She didn't want Kip to ruin it. She put it in her carry-sack.

Then she set off again and walked faster, taking deep breaths of the warm air.

After a time, she stopped and took her flute out.

She wasn't hiding now.

It would be all right to play as she walked.

She hadn't practiced in a long time. It would be good to warm up a little before she got to the town.

She tied the corners of her carry-sack together and slipped it over her shoulder.

Then she raised the flute to her lips.

Heart blew softly. Her hands were a little stiff at first. She kept playing. Soon her fingers flew over the silver metal. A tune as light as dandelion down floated into the air.

Kip ran ahead, then came back. He saw a squirrel and chased it. Heart could hear him crashing through the vines.

He came back panting, his tail high.

Heart lowered the flute to smile at him.

The first farm was around the next bend.

Heart waited until she was on the edge of the town to start playing again.

Then she walked straight to the market square.

People turned when they heard the flute.

Heart kept walking.

Some of the people followed her.

It was a pretty town.

The streets were clean.

Many people were dressed in velvet with shiny silver buttons.

No one wore rags—and they all smiled at her.

Heart found a place on a street corner by the square. She pulled the winter hat Ruth had given her from her carry-sack. She turned it upside-down and set it front of her.

Then she played.

She chose quick, lively tunes.

The notes rushed out, fast as creek water.

Heart danced. Kip sat up to beg. He rolled over and over. He walked on his hind legs. He did all the tricks he had learned from the Gypsies.

People laughed at Kip. They tapped their feet to the melodies. They applauded. They put pennies in the hat.

When she had enough, Heart stopped playing. She put the flute away and looked around.

There were a hundred market stalls. Most were selling wonderful food. Her mouth watered.

Heart bought cheese, fragrant, dark bread,

and a little box of butter. She bought a pair of new socks and some rosy apples. The butcher sold her a bone for Kip.

Heart put everything in her carry-sack.

Then she walked slowly out of the market place. Kip stayed close.

She turned down a long, narrow street.

It was shady.

Big trees arched over the houses. Heart saw a small cottage with a yard full of roses.

A tall, thin woman came out of the front door. She waved. "What a lovely dog!"

Kip trotted toward her. Heart stared. Tucked beneath the woman's arm was a paper-box like the one from Lord Dunraven's castle.

"What is that?" Heart asked politely, pointing.

The woman smiled. "A book. Haven't you ever seen a book?"

✦CHAPTER SIX

The woman's name was Toni Doohan. Her dark hair was a cloud around her face.

She held the book out, turning the leaves of paper. There were no pictures.

"This one was my great grandmother's," she told Heart. Heart smiled. Toni Doohan seemed very nice.

"It's about Yolen's Crossing," she added.

"Where is that?" Heart asked, puzzled.

Toni laughed and leaned down to pat Kip's head. "Here. This town is Yolen's Crossing. See?"

She turned the book toward Heart.

She ran her finger beneath some of the tiny patterns.

Heart met her eyes. "I don't understand."

Toni sighed. "Where are you from?"

Heart hesitated. If Lord Dunraven's men came looking they would ask people questions.

"A little village a long way from here," she said, finally.

Toni looked sad. "So many people never learn to read."

Heart blinked. "Read?"

Toni nodded. "Read. It's rare enough. But at least Lord Irmaedith doesn't forbid books the way most the others do."

Heart saw the anger in Toni's eyes.

"Listen," Toni said suddenly.

She opened the book.

She looked down at it and began speaking. "The two largest towns are now Yolen's Crossing and San Coville, farther west," she said. She kept talking.

She traced a zig-zag line with her finger as she spoke, sliding line by line down the paper.

It took Heart a long time to figure it out.

When she did, she got the shivers.

This was amazing! The little patterns were words somehow.

Toni could look at them and say them aloud!

Heart listened intently.

She watched Toni's eyes go back and forth.

The story began with the people who had come to this place long ago. A family named Yolen had been the first.

They had made a fine farm in the valley.

They had built the first little store and a flour mill on the river. Other farmers had come to settle. The book told their names and where they had lived.

"And then Talman Irmaedith was named lord of the land," Toni read.

Heart nodded to let Toni to know she was listening.

"He claimed the fields and mountains. He took a share of every harvest. He hunted the unicorns in the forests."

Heart made a little sound.

Toni glanced up.

Heart got a second set of shivers. Ash Grove's story had a unicorn in it, too, but no one had believed it.

"Please go on," she said quietly.

"You could learn to read it yourself," Toni said.

Heart swallowed. "Is it hard?"

Toni smiled. "A little. But it's worth it. I could teach you."

"Could you teach me right now?" Heart asked. She didn't want to leave the unicorns alone any longer than she had to.

Toni smiled. "It would take a few weeks to get you started."

Heart thought about the book in her carry-sack.

She longed to find out what it said about the rearing unicorns.

But she was afraid to show it to Toni.

She wanted to learn how to read too—but she couldn't stay for weeks.

She shouldn't stay even another hour.

"I have to go," she said sadly. "But thank you very much."

Toni closed the book and straightened. "You could come back tomorrow."

Heart looked at the ground.

"Are you staying on a farm near town? Would your family mind?" Toni asked.

Heart let out a careful breath. She couldn't tell this kind woman about the rearing unicorns—or where she was from, or anything else. She shouldn't even be talking to her.

"I can't," she said carefully. "But thank you very much."

Toni sighed, then nodded, then tapped the book with one graceful finger. "This book was written by a woman who died two hundred years ago."

Heart was amazed. She started to ask who the woman had been and how she'd made all the little marks so neatly.

Then the sound of hoofbeats made her turn.

Two men had turned their horses down the lane. They were riding at a clattering trot.

They wore dark shirts.

Both had crossbows and swords.

Toni slid the book into a pocket in her skirt. She nodded at the riders.

Heart glanced at the men as they passed.

"Lord Irmaedith is sending his men all the way past San Coville," Toni said once they were gone. "No one seems to know why." She twirled the clover between two fingers. "Have you heard anything about it?"

Heart didn't answer for a moment. Then she stepped back. "I have to go," she repeated.

Toni nodded. "Come back any time. I will teach you to read."

Heart smiled and thanked her again.

She called Kip, and they headed back toward the main road.

She would walk out of town the way she had come in.

If she saw Lord Irmaedith's men again they

would think she was a farm girl, just as Toni had.

Heart could feel the corner of the book pressing against her back.

She had to learn to read somehow.

She had to find out what it said about the rearing unicorns. Maybe the book would tell her where her family lived.

But first she had to get as far away from Lord Dunraven and the rumors about Moonsilver as she could.

Maybe in San Coville she could find someone to help.

Heart walked faster.

✦CHAPTER SEVEN

Heart kept going. She tried to travel fast.

It was hard to keep the unicorns hidden, but they seemed to understand that they had to stay where the forest was thickest.

Heart played her flute in two tiny mountain villages.

The people were poor. They gave her food instead of pennies. They tossed Kip bits of meat from their own dinners.

Then the roads began to lead downhill and the land leveled out. The river Heart followed was wide and lazy.

Every day more people and wagons passed on the road.

Heart could see them in glimpses through the trees.

There were farmers' wagons.

People in fancy carriages went by too.

The women wore long dresses and hats with flowers and feathers.

There were people leading cows and goats too. Their clothes were clean and plain.

"San Coville must be a big town," Heart said to Avamir. "All kinds of people are going there."

The unicorn mare tossed her head.

The Gypsy bells jingled.

Then they jingled again.

Heart stared. Avamir hadn't tossed her head a second time. The bells sounded again, distant and silvery. Heart turned to peer through the branches.

There was no one on the road.

"You're imagining it," she told herself.

Moonsilver reached out to nudge her shoulder with his muzzle. An instant later the sound of tiny Gypsy bells came again.

Heart peeked out of the trees. Moonsilver and Avamir followed. They stood close behind her.

Kip wagged his tail, his ears raised forward.

"That's Binney's wagon!" Heart breathed.

The whole caravan of bright-colored wagons was coming around a bend in the road. Heart ached to run toward her friends, but she knew she couldn't.

"Stay back," she said to the unicorns. "We'll just wait until they pass."

Kip barked.

"Hush," Heart scolded him. He barked again.

Heart reached down to hold him back, but it was already too late. Kip bounded out of the trees.

Heart covered her mouth with one hand. She could only watch as Kip streaked toward the road.

She heard the shouts when Binney spotted Kip. He raced in circles around Sadie, Fiona's dog.

The Gypsies reined in their ponies. They lined up along the edge of the road, shading their eyes, looking out over the meadow.

Heart ducked back into the trees. "We would only bring them harm," she began, but Avamir pawed at the ground with a forehoof. Moonsilver reared, striking at the air. Then they

walked past Heart into the open meadow.

On the road the Gypsies saw them and cheered.

Binney waved joyously. Josepha and Talia shouted Heart's name, their hands cupped around their mouths.

Heart felt her eyes flood with tears.

She stepped out of the trees and waved.

Whistles and cheers made her grin.

The Gypsies found a gentle enough slope and one by one the wagons lurched down it and into the meadow.

Once the wagons were stopped in their usual neat circle, Binney jumped down.

"Binney!" Heart cried out. She ran toward the Gypsy woman.

"Oh, we missed you," Binney said. She swung Heart off her feet and turned in a circle.

When Binney set her down Heart saw Davey smiling at her. Behind him Zim was grinning.

"They are beautiful," Binney said, looking at the unicorns. "I love watching them. And I will always be grateful to Moonsilver for saving Davey."

Heart smiled at her. "I missed all of you so much."

"The rumors have run this way," Binney told her.

"I know," Heart said.

Binney glanced up at the sky. "We have an hour before sunset." She raised her chin and her voice. "A celebration tonight! Our dear Heart has come back to us."

Heart smiled at her, then glanced at Avamir and Moonsilver. They were moving back into the trees. It would be all right if they stayed with the Gypsies for a night or two, she thought.

She was so glad to be with them.

It felt wonderful to be with people who cared about her, people who loved Kip and Moonsilver and Avamir.

That night it was chilly. Kip curled up between the unicorns behind a copse of trees.

Heart slept soundly in Binney's wagon.

Her dreams were shadowy and dark.

The mountains she ran in were steep and bleak.

When she cried out, Binney reached out to soothe her.

✦CHAPTER EIGHT

For two days the Gypsies traveled the road. Heart and the unicorns walked along a wooded creek that ran below it.

Kip ran back and forth between them.

Heart told the Gypsies everything that had happened to her—except for the part about accidentally stealing the book.

She wanted to show it to them.

She decided not to.

It would only put them in more danger.

She didn't want Lord Dunraven to be able to blame the Gypsies for *anything*.

The next morning they came to a village.

Heart and the unicorns went around it.

They all met on the other side.

When they stopped for noon dinner Davey brought Heart a bowl of sweet, spicy beans. They were steaming hot and delicious.

"A woman in that last town said Lord Irmaedith's men rode through yesterday."

Heart set down the bowl.

Davey's eyes were deep and sad.

Avamir stopped grazing and lifted her head.

Heart sighed. "We should leave today. We should get as far away from you as we can."

Davey shrugged unhappily. "I almost wish Moonsilver wasn't a real unicorn."

Heart felt an idea bloom inside her. "Davey," she began carefully, "if they found a fake unicorn, they'd stop looking for a real one."

Trembling with hope, she pulled the goat horn from her carry sack.

Davey turned it over in his hands.

He looked up, puzzled.

"We can teach the act to Avamir," Heart said. "At the next show, you can pretend to fall and she can touch you and—"

"That's it!" Davey shouted. "I'll tell Binney."

Heart watched him splash across the little creek as he headed back toward the wagons.

Avamir sidled closer. She lowered her head to sniff at the goat horn.

"Will you stand for sticky pine gum on your forehead?" Heart asked her.

Avamir wrinkled her upper lip.

Heart laughed.

Moonsilver came close, reaching over Heart's head to nuzzle his mother's shoulder.

Heart stepped back and watched them.

Moonsilver was tall now, nearly as tall as Avamir.

Avamir was still a good mother, kind and gentle.

Moonsilver wasn't timid anymore, though.

"Performing with the Gypsies cured your shyness," Heart told him. Then she laughed again. "And mine, I think."

The next day, walking, Heart made up a tune for Avamir's act.

By midmorning the unicorn mare understood perfectly.

Heart saved bits of bread from her noontime meal.

Every time she played the tune she tossed a piece to Kip. By evening he had learned to come when he heard the new melody.

The next morning, Avamir and Kip both came running when Heart played the tune. Avamir raced with Kip, just as Moonsilver had.

Moonsilver watched them practice for a while. Then he wandered off to graze

Heart liked the new melody. It was a slower, more serious melody than the one Kip had liked.

It fit Avamir better.

As they walked, Heart kept glancing up the slope to the road.

It felt wonderful to be with the Gypsies again.

Playing the flute made her feel happy.

Heart kissed Moonsilver on the muzzle as he

and Avamir settled in to sleep that evening. Kip lay between them as usual.

Heart walked up to the Gypsy camp.

By the bright campfire, she explained her idea to Binney.

"Avamir is nearly trained," Heart finished.

"In two days?" Binney asked.

Heart smiled.

Binney nodded thoughtfully. "It'll work, I think. We'll be in San Coville in four days. Will you be ready by then?"

"Of course she will," Zim said from behind Binney.

Heart nodded, grinning.

The firelight flickered, lighting the Gypsies' faces.

"Heart, watch!" Talia called.

Talia and Joseph had learned how to balance full pitchers of water on their heads.

Heart played them a slow, graceful melody.

Talia and Josepha danced in gliding circles.

Their arms rose and fell.

Their fingers and hands seemed to dance.

The water in the pitchers swayed gently.

"Will you play for us in San Coville?" Talia asked.

Heart nodded.

"We made the most beautiful shawls to wear," Josepha told her.

"I have more cloth," an older woman said from the fireside. "I'll stitch one for Heart."

Heart recognized her. It was Talia's aunt—the one who had loaned her a costume in Derrytown.

It seemed so long ago.

Heart raised the flute and began to play.

Her sleeve slid up over her wrist.

The silver sparkle of the bracelet was burnished into sunset colors by the firelight.

+CHAPTER NINE

All the way to San Coville, Heart rehearsed the act.

At first the horn wouldn't stay on Avamir's forehead at all.

Heart borrowed Davey's knife.

She hollowed out the horn until it was a light, thin shell that weighed almost nothing.

Then the pine tar worked.

Avamir could toss her head.

She could shake her mane.

The horn stayed in place.

When Kip chased Avamir around in a circle, she reared and looked magnificent.

Davey was practicing the fall.

He would use the low wire this time—and

of course he wouldn't really get hurt.

Avamir understood her part of the act the first time they practiced it.

"Well," Binney said. "All the old stories talk about unicorns healing people. She knows all about how to do that part."

In the evenings Heart played a dance melody for Talia and Josepha to practice. They decided it should start slowly, then speed up.

"You have gotten very good," Zim told her.

Heart smiled. Zim played so well. His praise made her blush.

"Do you think Moonsilver would get into a wagon and hide there while we put on our show?" Binney asked.

Heart's smile faded.

She had been so busy rehearsing that she hadn't given Moonsilver a single thought. "Maybe," she said slowly. "But maybe not."

"We could send someone to stay with him in the woods," Binney said. "But I'd rather have him close."

Heart nodded. "I'm just not sure he will understand."

"We had better see," Binney said. "We emptied Zim's second wagon is empty just now."

Heart nodded.

She walked back to the trees. Moonsilver was standing up, not yet asleep.

He followed her quietly to the wagons.

Avamir came with them. Her forehead was smudged with pine gum.

Heart watched Zim make sure there was nothing in the wagon.

Then she walked up the little ramp. "Moonsilver?" she asked quietly. "Would you mind coming inside here?"

The unicorn touched his muzzle to the ramp. He stretched out his neck, sniffing at the wagon gate.

Then he lowered his head and stepped up into the wagon.

There wasn't much room.

Heart scrambled out of his way.

Moonsilver stood calmly while Zim closed up the back of the wagon.

"We'll fill it with sweet straw and fresh grass when we get to San Coville," Binney said.

Moonsilver nickered.

Everyone laughed.

Zim opened the wagon gate and Moonsilver backed out. He nuzzled Heart's cheek, then went off to sleep beside his mother and Kip. Heart yawned.

"Bed for you, too," Binney said. "We'll make sure we get to San Coville at dusk to be safe."

✦CHAPTER TEN

San Coville's green was wide and sloped. The people sat uphill from the circle of lanterns.

Moonsilver had ridden into town inside the wagon.

He stood quietly, eating the grass Heart had gathered.

When the show started Heart watched the other acts.

It was amazing how many new tricks the Gypsies had added.

Talia and Josepha danced to her flute music.

The audience clapped and clapped.

Heart swirled her shawl as they all three bowed.

The other acts went on.

Binney made jokes. Everyone laughed.

Then came the last act.

Heart held her breath, standing next to Avamir in the dark. Inside the ring of lanterns Davey and the other jugglers began.

They threw their clubs high in the air.

Their hands blurred in the lantern light.

Then Davey walked out on the low wire. He threw the clubs high, walking forward.

Then he pretended to lose his balance.

He dropped the clubs, then fell sideways, catching the wire and swinging himself back up.

The audience gasped in relief.

But then Davey dropped to the ground. He landed for just an instant on his feet, then sprawled on the ground, his eyes closed.

It looked very real.

The audience gasped, then groaned.

They thought he was really hurt.

"Go ahead," Heart said to Avamir. She nudged the mare's side.

Avamir galloped forward, and the audience

made a low sighing sound when they saw her.

She bent to touch her goat horn to Davey's lips. He slowly opened his eyes and stood up.

Heart walked forward then, playing her flute.

Avamir galloped in graceful circles as they had practiced. Kip ran alongside her.

Then Heart changed melodies, and they both came to her.

Avamir had even learned to bow like Moonsilver had.

The audience stood up, whooping and clapping.

"Psssst!"

Heart looked around to see Binney gesturing to the side of the field.

There, standing in the shadows, were five or six men in dark clothes. The lantern light glinted from their sword scabbards. They were laughing, shaking their heads.

Heart grinned. Perfect. Lord Irmaedith's men had seen the whole thing.

She walked to their side of the field and

played the melody again. Avamir and Kip ran to her.

She patted Avamir's neck and reached up to the goat horn.

The pine gum was working perfectly, but she pretended to press the horn in place.

She could hear the men laughing behind her.

Across the field, she saw Binney grin.

She led Avamir and Kip out to bow again.

Then she and Zim played a lively tune as people left.

Heart couldn't stop smiling.

"They'll tell everyone that the unicorn is a fake," Davey said happily. "You can stay with us."

"Let's camp outside town," Binney shouted. "I know a good meadow close to the road."

All the Gypsies went about their work.

Heart was grateful. They were tired, but they knew Moonsilver would hate being cooped up all night. And the truth was they all liked the open country better than any town.

The wagons rolled onto the road.

Binney knew exactly where the field was.

The fire was made quickly.

Supper was warm bread and apples.

Moonsilver and Avamir grazed quietly in the dark behind the wagons.

After supper everyone else went to bed, but Heart stayed by the fire playing quietly.

She was too relieved and too happy to go to sleep.

Zim came to stand beside her.

He played a melody that danced with hers.

Heart closed her eyes and lost herself in the music.

"I wonder if anyone in my family plays," she said after they let the song drift into silence.

"Where are they?" he asked.

Heart shrugged. "All I can remember is Simon Pratt finding me."

Zim stared into the fire. "He's the one you followed to Dunraven's castle?"

Heart nodded. "I want to find my family."

"You should learn to read," Zim said.

Heart blinked, startled. "Read?"

He nodded. "My mother could. There are books that tell about different towns, about the families who settled them."

"Can you read?" Heart asked, trying to keep her voice even.

Zim shrugged. "Not really. A little, maybe."

Heart pressed her lips together. "Will you keep a secret?"

Zim nodded somberly. "All Gypsies know how to keep secrets."

Heart ran to get the book. She took it out of her carry-sack without waking Binney.

Coming back, she glanced around the camp.

No one else was awake.

"I didn't mean to take it," Heart began. She opened the book to the drawing and held it out to Zim. "It's the same design as the embroidering on my blanket."

Zim arched his eyebrows. "It is?"

Heart nodded. "Exactly. But you can't tell Binney or anyone else about the book, Zim."

He frowned. "None of us would tell an outsider."

"But if Dunraven's men ever question them, they don't have to lie if they don't know anything," Heart insisted.

Zim nodded slowly. "I won't tell anyone else."

He looked at the rearing unicorns. Then he placed his finger beneath the tiny patterns. He squinted and stared, then made sounds that seemed not to be words at first.

"Th . . . th . . . the," he said. "The."

Heart watched his eyes. They didn't go back and forth like Toni's had. They were glued to a single word as he tried to puzzle it out.

"The M . . . m . . . The Mooo, Moun . . . Mount . . . t . . . t . . . t . . . tain . . . tains?" Zim said. He looked up at her, then back at the book. "Then it says o . . . o . . . of . . . Of. Th . . . the . . . M . . . M . . . Moun . . . Moun . . . tains of th . . . the . . . mmmm . . ." He stopped and looked at the sky, then took a big breath and started over on the last word. "Mo . . . No. Moun . . . No, it is mooo . . . then . . . nnnn.

Moon." He looked up, smiling.

Heart waited, holding her breath.

"The Mountains of the Moon," he said slowly. Then he frowned. "That must be wrong, Heart. It makes no sense at all."

Heart stood completely still.

In her dreams the mountains were the color of the full moon. Did the book say something about her dreams?

"Have you ever heard of The Mountains of the Moon?" Heart asked.

Zim shrugged. "No. But, Heart, you need someone who can truly read. Gypsies don't. My mother was a town woman. She taught me a little, but I've forgotten most of it."

"Try again," Heart pleaded.

Zim tried.

He wrinkled his face and stared at the book.

He pushed his finger back and forth over the same place a dozen times.

"Th . . . the . . . A . . . A . . . A . . . A . . . An . . . An . . . ," he began. Then he looked up. "It's a long word. I can't remember enough of the letters." He stared at it again.

"Letters?" Heart echoed.

"That's what the little designs are called. Letters." He handed the book back to her. "I'm sorry, Heart."

Heart hugged him. "I love you all so much," she said, not knowing that she was going to say it.

"Everyone missed you," Zim said. Then he smiled. "Avamir and Moonsilver are lucky that you found them. And Kip."

He rose and stretched.

As he walked toward his wagon Heart glanced up at the sky.

Zim had done his best.

She would have to learn to read—somehow.

She smiled up at the sky. At least she could travel with the Gypsies now.

That meant she might be able to find someone who knew something about the drawing of the rearing unicorns.

It might lead her to her family. To her real home.

"Home."

Heart whispered the word as Zim started off to bed.

It was a magic word for her.

Heart turned toward Binney's wagon.

Past it, on the horizon, the moon was rising. It was almost full again. Heart watched it. The bracelet on her wrist felt snug and warm against her skin.

She breathed in the chilly night air.

The unicorns were asleep and so was Kip. They were all safe for now. And her family would help her. All she had to do was find them.